Modern Curriculum Press
BEGINNING
TO
READ
Series

The Three Bears

The Three Bears

Margaret Hillert

illustrated by Irma Wilde

MODERN CURRICULUM PRESS
Cleveland • Toronto

Copyright © 1963, by Modern Curriculum Press, Inc. Original copyright © 1963, by Follett Publishing Company, a division of Follett Corporation. All rights reserved. No part of this book may be reproduced in any form without written permission from the publisher. Manufactured in the United States of America.

ISBN 0-8136-5015-1 (hardbound)
ISBN 0-8136-5515-3 (paperback)

3 4 5 6 7 8 9 10   88 87 86 85

See the house.

It is red and yellow.

It is a funny little house.

7

One, two, three.

One is the father.

One is the mother.

One is the baby.

The father is big.

The baby is little.

See Mother work.

Mother can make something.

Away we go.

Away, away, away.

11

I can play.

My ball is blue.

See it go up.

Oh, look.

Here is a little house.

A funny little house.

I can go in.

Here is something.

Red, yellow, and blue.

One is big.

One is little.

14

I want something.

Here is one for me.

Here is something.

Red, yellow, and blue.

One is big.

One is little.

16

Here is one for me.

Here is something.

Red, yellow, and blue.

One is big.

One is little.

Here is one for me.

Here we come.

We can go in.

Father said, "Oh, oh!"

Mother said, "Oh, my!"

Baby said, "Oh, look!
It is not here."

Father said, "Oh, oh!"

Mother said, "Oh, my!"

Baby said, "Oh, look!

It is down."

Father said, "Oh, oh!"

Mother said, "Oh, my!"

Baby said, "Oh, look!
I see something."

24

Help, help!

I can jump down.

I can run.

Oh, Mother, Mother.

Here I come!

Modern Curriculum Press Beginning-To-Read Books

Margaret Hillert, author of several books in the MCP Beginning-To-Read Series, is a writer, poet, and teacher.

The Three Bears

Children will find new enjoyment in this favorite tale, beautifully illustrated, and with a text that uses 45 preprimer words.

Word List

7	see		mother	**13**	oh
	the		baby		look
	house				here
	it	**9**	big		in
	is				
	red	**10**	work		
	and		can	**15**	want
	yellow		make		for
	a		something		me
	funny				
	little	**11**	away	**20**	come
			we		
			go	**22**	said
					not
		12	I		
			play	**23**	down
8	one		my		
	two		ball	**25**	help
	three		blue		run
	father		up		jump

28